SUMMER ADVENTURE

The Beginning

Timm Fischer

The Reading Glass Books
(888) 420-3050
www.readingglassbooks.com
fulfillment@readingglassbooks.com

Table of Contents

CHAPTER 1

It was the last day of school, and Patrick and all his friends were excited to start their summer vacation. All the students at Garden Elementary School were talking about the plans they had for summer vacation. Patrick's friend John was talking about playing video games all summer and just relaxing. Patrick thought that might have been fun, but his family had other plans. Patrick was thinking he could play video games and watch TV all summer. He would love to hang out with his friends. But his family had other ideas.

Sara, Patrick's sister, was more adventurous than Patrick. She was excited about the mystery and the sense of exploration. Sara had always been excited to learn about new places; she had always wanted to visit the places she read about in a book. Sara often wrote and loved to write about things she had experienced.

Patrick and Sara's family never discussed with them what the plans were, but they said it will be enriching and exciting. They were from a small town in the middle of Missouri; they had never really been outside of Central Missouri.

"All right, friends, I have one more assignment for you before the bell rings," said the teacher.

"But it's summer break," cried out all the students in Ms. Duran's fourth grade class.

"Now hang on, friends, and listen. This assignment will not be hard," said Miss Duran. "In fact, the assignment is really easy. Are you ready for your assignment?" asked Ms. Duran.

"Yes, Ms. Duran," said all the children in unison.

"Okay then..." Ms. Duran paused and waited 'til right before the bell rang to dismiss the class. "All right... your assignment... is to... have a wonderful summer break."

Ring. Ring. Ring. The sound of the dismissal bell had always been deafening, but it was the sound of freedom and no homework.

As Patrick and Sara sprang from their desks, they could here chattering in the halls. It was the other students chatting about plans for summer break. They were chatting about movies and video games, and two girls were talking about where they are going for vacation. One girl said, "Well, I am going to Japan."

The other girl replied with, "Oh, that is nothing, we went there two summers ago. We are going to Australia this summer."

Out of what seemed like nowhere, another girl chimed in, "Did those egos come with the yachts?"

Sara laughed at that remark and at the same time got a little jealous but reminded herself that she was going on a vacation with her family. Not knowing where yet, she was full of anticipation as to where the destination would be. Sara thought maybe it would be Japan or Australia or maybe somewhere even more exotic like the Congo. She had read about all those places and always wanted to visit them.

Sara and Patrick grabbed their backpacks and were on their way to the bus. As they were about to head out, Ms. Duran stopped them. "Where are you two going?" asked Ms. Duran.

"To the bus to go home, Ms. Duran," replied Patrick.

"Yeah, Ms. Duran, our parents said we can't miss the bus this time. We can't be late," said Sara.

Ms. Duran responded with, "Oh, you won't be late, your parents are already here to pick you up." Ms. Duran went on to say, "Don't forget your assignment, I want a full report on your travels. Now go have fun, you two."

Patrick was not too pleased to hear that their parents were at the school to pick him and his sister up. With a grimacing look on his face, Patrick turned around and started to head to the front where his and his sister's parents were waiting for them.

They took their backpacks off as their mom and dad greeted them. "Hello, children!" first greeted by their mom then by their dad.

"Hello," said the children.

"How was your last day of school for the year?" asked their mom.

"It was okay," said Sara.

"It was boring," said Patrick.

"Well, are we all set then?" asked their dad.

"I think we are," replied their mom.

"Aren't we going home first?" asked Patrick.

Their mom replied with, "Nope, we are headed straight for fun and adventure."

Patrick thought, *How lame. It's more fun playing games with my friends.*

"Our first stop, children, is Mark Twain National Forest," said their dad. He went on to say, "It is 1.5 million acres of beautiful landscape, which anyone can enjoy. We can go hiking, mountain biking, fishing, and so much more."

"It would be fun to ride our bikes through the forest. Don't you agree, Patrick?" asked Sara.

Patrick kinda nodded and was not interested in going anywhere; he wanted to just sit back relax and play his favorite video game with his friends.

"Will we be able to explore all of the trails?" asked Sara.

"Yeah, maybe you will get lost in the forest. Yay, no more bratty sister!" exclaimed Patrick.

The children's mom added, "The forest has over 750 miles of trails. Some of the Ozark Trail winds through the forest. It also has streams, suitable for floating, canoeing, and kayaking. So no, Sara, we will not have time to explore that much trail. I am sorry."

In a sarcastic way, Patrick replied, "If we have to go somewhere for vacation, why couldn't it be someplace cooler like Japan or Australia?"

"You were listening to those girls talking in the hall, weren't you?" asked Sara.

"No... well, yes, kinda," replied Patrick. "I just thought if we were going to go somewhere, let's go somewhere where we could see something neat."

"Those girls are from a wealthy, prominent family." Sara went on to say, "Their heads are stuck in the clouds."

As Sara and Patrick's dad drove, Sara noticed the trees were getting thicker along the edge of the road. The brush was getting more dense, deeper, richer greens. The wildflowers were brilliant white and yellow, with blue and purple flowers scattered among the white and yellow flowers. There were trees with red flowers, white flowers, pink flowers, and trees with white bark; it reminded her of some of the pictures in the nature books that she reads. The shadows were starting to become more defined and more abundant.

Sara and Patrick's dad turned off the interstate onto a highway, though after a few miles on the highway, it seemed more like a country back road. The road had become more hilly and curvy. As the SUV rounded one bend, another bend was fast-approaching. As one hill was crested, there was another just on the other side. The trees seemed as if they were trying to reach out and shake hands to say hello. After what seemed like forever, they finally turned onto a gravel road that stretched far beyond what the eye can see. The trees were now even thicker and more lush than before. The undergrowth of the forest looked as if it had been untouched. The deeper they went, the more excited Sara was to explore and see what is out in the wilderness.

THUD! Sara was enjoying the view when a loud thud was heard from under the SUV. At the same time, the vehicle bounced, startling Sara.

CHAPTER 2

Patrick was playing a game on his phone; he didn't see what made the forest and nature so exciting. Leveling up on his video game was the excitement and thrilling adventures he sought. There just seemed to be an endless number of trees. The road was windy and hilly, made him queasy. The trees seemed to be mocking him with their branches outreached, as if they wanted to grab him and pull him into the dense thick forest. The road was increasingly getting narrower, hillier, and windier than when they first turned onto the highway, which seemed more like a back woods road that doesn't get traveled on often. Returning to his phone, he thought he would just play his game and not worry about the road. After what seemed like hours of driving down this windy road, Patrick and Sara's dad turned off onto a gravel road. The road got bumpy from the rocks that make up the road and from the ruts made from water runoff washing out the road. It was too bumpy for Patrick to continue playing his game on the phone so he switched to listening to music on his phone. After a few miles down the gravel road, he lost signal, his music cut off.

THUD! The hard bump that hit the SUV caused his earbuds to pop out of his ears.

"What was that?" asked Patrick.

"Oh, just a rut in the road," replied their dad.

"That scared me," said Sara.

"Don't let it... ," their dad started to say.

Thump, thump, thump, thump. As the SUV continued down the road, the thumping sounds continued and became more apparent. Sara and Patrick's dad started to push in on the brake then slowly pulled over on the side of the road. As their dad slowed down, the thumping sound started to slow down. Once the SUV came to a complete stop, so did the thumping sound.

"That sounds like more than a bump in the road, Dad," said Sara. "That hard thud scared me."

"Is that a flat tire, Dad?" asked Patrick.

"I hope not," said their dad.

"I will take care of it," said their mom.

Everyone looked at the mom, as if asking her, "What are you talking about?"

Their mom replied, "What? You look as if I don't know what I am doing."

Their mom had worked on vehicles all her childhood and into her adult life. She had done everything, from rebuilding an engine to rebuilding transmissions and from repairing body damage to general maintenance. Their mom got out and looked around to see what they hit. In the distance, she saw what could be a pothole. *The tire can wait for now*, she thought.

She wanted to investigate the cause of the large thud and the tire going flat. As she started to walk down the road to investigate what caused the flat, their dad got out of the SUV.

"Is there something wrong honey?" asked the dad.

The mom replied, "No, it was just a washout in the road. Let's get the tire changed and get back on our way."

Sara said to Patrick, "Mom has a puzzled look on her face. I wonder if something is wrong. It looks as if she had seen a ghost."

"Hmmm, I don't know," replied Patrick.

"Well, do you think we should ask if everything is all right?"

"I think we should just ignore it."

"Why?"

With a stern look on Patrick's face, he replied, "Because you know how Mom gets when people 'intervene.'"

"I would not exactly call asking Mom if she is okay 'intervening,' now would you?"

"I dunno." Patrick returned to trying to get phone signal. "Why isn't this thing working? Grrr!"

"It is from all the trees. They are blocking cell signal," said Sara.

On the outside of the car, Mom tightened down the last lug nut and lowered the SUV back onto the ground.

"All done," said Mom. "Let's get back on the road."

"That was not hard! I did not know you knew how to do that," said Dad.

"No, it's not, let's just get on our way," said Mom with a startled look on her face.

Back on the road, Sara could not stop thinking about the look on her mom's face. It was a face of concern and distraught. Sara was really concerned for her mom and what she had found in the rut of the road. Dad didn't seem concerned. However, he didn't look into the rut. And Patrick was just being Patrick, trying to get his phone to work. She was wondering what her mom saw in the rut in the road.

"I don't have a good feeling about this road," said Patrick.

"Do you know where we are?" asked Sara.

"Yes," replied Dad.

"Honey, are you sure?" asked Mom.

"Yes! See, the GPS says we are heading the right way," replied Dad.

"Wait! You are using GPS?!" exclaimed Mom. She was thinking, *You heard Patrick complaining that he did not have signal. So if Patrick does not have signal on his phone, how do you have signal on yours? These woods are too dense with overhanging trees to get cell or regular GPS signal.*

"Yes, why?"

"You may want to double-check. Are you sure you have GPS right now?"

"Yes, I had it the last time I looked."

"When was that?" asked Mom.

"Right before we turned onto this road," said Dad.

"GPS will not work with all of these trees over hanging and blocking the signals," Mom replied.

"May we turn around and go back the way we came?" asked Patrick.

As the SUV went further down the road, the road started to get even more windy and hilly. The road got darker, the trees became more dense. The gravel road turned into a dirt road. The road seemed as if it had not been maintained in years. The road got bumpier and harder to maintain control of the SUV. The road narrowed, and the shoulder had disappeared.

"Hey, there is a sign up ahead. Let's see what it says," said Dad.

As he drove, the sign seemed as if it were moving further away, as did the narrowing of the road. As the SUV approached the sign, the road started to stop looking like a road and more like a dirt path. Now what once seemed like a two-lane road was now more of a one-lane driveway. The dirt became less pact and more loose and even harder to drive on.

The sign was made of what seemed like old barn wood painted white. It looked as if the boards on the sign were broken and not cut to make the sign. The sign came into view and very clear. There were holes sporadically throughout the sign and in big bold black letters read, "PRIVATE DRIVE"; under that read, "KEEP OUT."

"Dad, I think we should turn around and go back the same way we went. Maybe we missed a turn somewhere," Patrick stated.

"Let's just see if there is a house up here. We will ask for directions," Dad replied.

Quickly approaching was another sign made of the same broken wood, painted with the same white paint, this time in red letters.

Dad said, "Hey, there is another sign, let's see what this one says. Maybe it is a road sign that will tell us how to get back on the main road."

"I doubt it, Dad, the last one said 'PRIVATE DRIVE, KEEP OUT,'" replied Sara.

"Well, let's just see if there is a house up here, maybe they can help," Dad replied.

"This is a little bit out of the way of civilization, would you agree?" Mom asked Dad.

"Well, someone must live here. After all, someone had to have put up those signs."

"That maybe so, but I am still uncomfortable being out here, especially with the children."

The sign appeared clear and read in big, bold, red letters, "WARNING: KEEP OUT"; under that read, "PRIVATE PROPERTY."

"Dad, someone clearly wants... ," started to say Sara, then came Sara's high-pitched, shrilling scream. "AHHH!"

"What is it, honey?" asked Dad.

"There... was... a... man... He... was st-standing... right behind that tree by the sign."

"Are you sure? What did he look like? I don't see him."

"I am telling you, I saw him standing there. He was tall, thin, had a brown worn-out hat that looked kinda like what a cowboy would wear. He had a dark brown mustache and a scraggly goatee. You have to believe me."

"Look, there is a house just up the road, it's not that far. I will drive up there and see if anyone is home. I will ask for directions and get us out of here," replied Dad.

"Why can't we just turn around and go back the same way we came?" asked Sara.

"I believe you, honey," said Mom with a startled look on her face.

"Did no one else see him?" Sara silently asking herself. "There is that same look on Mom's face. What did she see in the rut in the road? Why are there signs in what we think is a public access road?" Sara has a lot of questions, but she knows there are no answers to them at the moment.

Chapter 3

Dad pulled up to the house at the top of the drive. The house was a three-story colonial white house but worn down. It looks as if it was in dire need of maintenance. The shutters were hanging on by one hinge, and the white paint was peeling off. The front porch looked as if it would collapse at any moment. The second-story balcony looked a little more stable but not by much; it as well was in need of desperate repair. The white fence surrounding the house was missing slats. The grass in the yard was brown with bald patches throughout. The dry, dusty patches in the yard made it look as if it were a desert.

"That house looks like something from a horror movie!" exclaimed Sara.

"It is just a rundown old house, there is nothing to be afraid of," replied Dad.

"Do you really think someone lives in that old rundown, rat-infested, mold-growing house?"

"It may look like that from the outside, but we have not been on the inside. Remember, Sara, do not judge a book by its cover."

"Yeah, Sara, you read all the time, you should know that. Besides, you are a fraidy cat and even a fly will startle you," Patrick said in the most obnoxious way.

"Well, it's not that I am afraid or scared, but it is more like it looks like no one is living there..." After a short pause, she continued on to say, "If there is no one here, no matter what, let's turn around and just head the same way we came. I am sure we will be able to at least find the highway traveling the same way we came."

As Dad approached the house on foot, he could hear his wife yelling at him from the SUV, "Let's just turn around and go back the same way, it is starting to get dark!"

"Come on, Dad, please can we just leave?" asked Sara. Sara continued to say to her mom, "I feel as if we are being watched."

Halfway to the house, Dad decided to turn around and head back to the SUV. Taking advice from his wife and Sara, he made the decision to head back out the same way he drove in. He turned the SUV around and headed down the road in the opposite direction. When they passed the second sign that read, "WARNING: KEEP OUT" and "PRIVATE PROPERTY" under that, Sara and Mom looked out the rearview mirror and saw the tall man with the beard standing right behind the sign.

"See, there he is, I told you someone was standing there!" exclaimed Sara.

"I saw him, honey, I believe you," Mom replied.

Patrick nor Dad saw the tall thin man with a beard. By the time they looked, the man had already disappeared into the shadows.

"There is no one there!" exclaimed Patrick.

"GRRR! Well, Mom saw him too, so don't claim that I am seeing things again nor claim that I am a fraidy cat."

Sara's face turned beet red, her nose wrinkled up, and her eyebrows lowered. Sara was mad that that comment was made. Sara's brother was always calling her a fraidy cat and never believing her, even when the proof was right in front of his face. Patrick had always said that Sara was making stuff up, that she was scared of everything, that her nose was always stuck in a book, and that her head was in the clouds and not down on earth.

"That's enough, Patrick, stop antagonizing your sister. I saw what she saw," said Mom.

Dad drove slower and more carefully over the rut to avoid hitting it as hard this time. Dad thought, *As soon as we get into a town, we need to get that tired fixed or replaced. It is always a good thing to have a spare tire available. But for now, we just need to get to the campsite and get some rest.*

As Dad drove, Mom took out a map of the of the area and said, "GPS is not working in this area, we are going back to the old-school method." She looked on the map and found the road they drove down and followed it to the last place they turned and noticed that there was a turn they should have made to connect to the road leading into the park. "Turn left at the next road." The GPS did not show the road on the map.

"It is getting dark. Are we going to have enough time to set up camp?" asked Sara.

"Yes, plus we have lanterns," replied Dad.

The road didn't seem to have existed when Dad was driving down the road the first time. Turning onto the road leading to the national park seemed much more inviting than the road leading to the house.

Sara was wondering why the tall, thin man was standing behind the sign. After thinking about it, it looked as if he was waving his arms in the air. Also, why did he seem to have been saying something? Sara was wondering what he was saying, if he was saying anything. She was wondering what the look on Mom's face was about. She looked startled and acted as if there was something wrong.

Patrick was wondering why they didn't stop for the man that was yelling and waving his arms in the air. It looked as if the man was trying to stop them. Patrick didn't want his sister to know that he saw the man. He didn't want Sara to have the satisfaction that she was right and that she saw the man earlier. He also wanted her to remain scared of the woods. Patrick just wanted to go home and play video games with his friends. He also felt that he was missing out on a lot of movie-watching time. He could read about anywhere they go. He kept thinking about the video game he was programing with his friends and wondering how the project was coming along.

Dad was wondering why Sara and his wife were the only ones who saw the tall, thin man. He was also wondering how he missed the turn onto the road. Dad was wondering why the GPS didn't pick up the road that he had missed. He was grateful that his wife picked up the map the last time they stopped at a refueling station.

Mom was wondering why the rut was in the road and why the object in the rut was there. On the way down to the house, Sara saw a tall, thin man with a beard and mustache. Why was she the only one to see him? On the way back from the house, Sara and she were the only people who saw the man, which Mom was thinking, *That is odd.* Mom also thought about how it was strange that the man appeared to be waving his arms, almost as if he was trying to flag them down. So far, none of this made any sense. Why was the house in such dire need of repair? It looked as if someone might be living in the house.

CHAPTER 4

About an hour of driving, Dad finally arrived at the check-in point to get the camping spot.

The camping spot was secluded and surrounded by trees, with a soft patchy spot in the grass, perfect for setting up tents. There was one tent that was an easy-pop-up double-sleeper and two single pop-up sleepers, perfect for each camper. The tents were set up by lantern light.

A tarp under the tent acted as a moisture barrier. The tarp also acted as a barrier between the cold ground and the floor of the tent. On the top of the tent was another piece made of the same material as the tent, called a rain fly. The rain fly protected the campers from any moisture that might come in brought about by rain or drizzle and for airflow to keep the inside of the tent cooler. There was a built-in mosquito netting so a camper could open up flaps to allow air to circulate into the tent while keeping mosquitoes and other flying insects out.

"Let's get some rest, we have a busy day tomorrow," said Dad.

"Good night, everyone," said Mom.

"Good night," Patrick and Sara said in unison.

As everyone started to fall asleep, they could hear all the nocturnal creatures making their calls. The wind blowing made the night cooler and the air more moist. After such a long day of driving and just simply traveling, they were all tired and were asleep within minutes of lying down.

Far less traffic and lights, the night was much darker in the forest than in the city, there was far less noise pollution, and it was easier to breathe. There was also far less air, water, and land pollution.

The cicadas, crickets, and owls were playing their nocturnal music; while loud, it was also relaxing and calming. As the sun started to rise, the reds, oranges, and yellows began to paint the sky. The morning light was unobstructed by buildings, bridges, and other unnatural objects. The nocturnal creatures began to become silent. And the diurnal animals began to sing their songs and start their morning routines.

CHAPTER 5

Sara was the first to rise; she got out of her tent and felt the cool soft grass against her bare feet. The morning dew made the grass glisten as the sun's rays beamed down on it, making the water droplets sparkle. She could identify some of the plants, like daffodils, walnut trees, and birch trees. She wished she knew more than she did. She studied plants and animals, but there were stark differences between pictures in a book and viewing it naturally. Sara noticed a sign on a trailhead and was excited about taking a hike.

As everyone else woke up, they noticed that Sara was walking around, looking at the trees and flowers. As they walked over to her, Sara turned around and said, "Good morning, can we go on a hike and explore the trails?"

"Sure, let's do that after breakfast," said Dad.

"Yay! I am hungry, this is exciting," said Sara.

"I will harvest some wild edibles, if you like," suggested Patrick.

"What? You know which plants are edible and which are not?" asked Sara.

"I am not a complete moron, I do study and read on occasion. School just bores me."

"So how about those edibles?" asked Dad. Dad went on to say, "Get me the right ingredients and I will make us some omelets."

"That sounds amazing. You have always been an excellent cook, it is like you can turn a piece of bark into a gourmet meal," teased Mom.

"With the right piece of bark, I can." Dad laughed.

As Patrick and Sara started to walk away, the voice of their mom rang out, "Stay together."

"Come on, Sara, let's gather some ingredients for omelets," said Patrick.

Patrick and Sara started around the campsite then took the trail. As they walked on the trail, Patrick pointed out some wild onions and wild garlic, along with some mushrooms on a decaying tree. Sara recognized the mushrooms from one of the many books she had read.

"That looks like oyster mushrooms," Patrick and Sara said in unison.

"Those might be great to sauté with the onions and garlic we found," suggested Patrick.

Back at the camp, Mom and Dad were building a fire and unpacking all the cooking equipment. The campsite had a spot to build a fire and cook. Dad gathered all the wood and arranged the wood in the form of a tepee to help the fire start easier. After gathering all the necessary cooking utensils and building the fire, Mom and Dad were waiting for Sara and Patrick to return.

"I haven't told you that in the rut, there was a piece of wood with a nail hammered through it. When you drove through the rut, the nail punctured the tire. It looks as if it was placed there purposefully. It is as if someone was waiting for someone to come along and hit the nail. However, the piece of wood was short, and it was broken off of something. If it was seen, it could have been easily avoided. So that leads to question if it was actually purposefully set there," said Mom.

"Is that why you looked so startled?" replied Dad.

"I tried to hide that. I didn't want to worry anyone because I was, and still am, unsure if that was purposefully placed."

"I don't think we really have anything to worry about. That house was old, and there was a ladder leaning up against the house. It looks as if it was being remodeled or refurbished. It looked like an old-style Victorian," Dad explained.

Sara and Patrick returned with the ingredients. Dad started by sautéing the mushrooms with the onions and garlic. He cracked open the eggs and started to assemble the omelets and finished cooking them.

"Wow, that was amazing! Thank you, Dad!" exclaimed Patrick and Sara.

"Yes, thank you, dear, that was amazing!" Mom exclaimed.

"May we go hiking now?!" Sara asked excitedly.

"Of course, let's choose a trail," said Dad.

"Hmmm... how about the Smith Creek Loop of Cedar Creek Trail?" said Sara.

"Sounds great," everyone agreed.

"This is one of many trails we can explore, this trail is short and great for a day hike," Mom read from the brochure.

"May I read the brochure later, Mom?" asked Sara.

"Of course, you may," replied Mom. "Now remember, we pack out what we back in. We will not leave even so much as a bubble gum wrapper," explained Mom.

On the trail, Sara spotted some deer, rabbits, and squirrels. The trail was inviting, and there was a spot in the trail that overlooked Cedar Creek from the bluffs. The beauty of the flowers, trees, and brush made the hike worth the trip. Sara was excited to have the opportunity to explore such a beautiful place. Secretly, Patrick was overwhelmed by the beauty of the flora and fauna of the area. He was also secretly excited to go on further adventures. He was excited to see what else Mark Twain National Forest had to offer.

It was a cooler summer day, in the 70s, and it was around lunchtime, and they were in a great spot overlooking the creek on top of the bluffs. The family decided to take out their lunch. While enjoying their lunch consisting of peanut-butter-and-jelly sandwiches and fresh celery and carrot sticks, Mom said, "Down there looks like a nice place to go fishing."

"We can go fishing in the creek, that would be fun," Dad said.

"Fishing, really?!" questioned Patrick.

"Yes, it can be relaxing and exciting at the same time," explained Dad.

After an enjoyable day of hiking and enjoying the scenery, the family finished the hike and returned to camp just in time to set up for a campfire and took out food to cook for dinner.

After dinner, they set around the fire to discuss the day's events and discussed what the plans for tomorrow were going to be. After a while of discussions, the agreed-upon plan was after breakfast, to pack a lunch and explore more and go fishing. The fishing trip would not be species-specific. It was just for the sake of relaxing and enjoying the nature around.

The next morning Sara was the first to wake. She founds the morning air refreshing and the cool grass under her feet soft and smooth. Sara loved the feel of the grass under her feet as well as the feel of the first rays from the sun against her face.

CHAPTER 6

Sara walked over to the trailhead and thought about taking a short hike before everyone else woke up, but as she was putting her shoes on, Patrick emerged from his tent and began to put his shoes on and walked over to Sara, asking her, "Are you planning on going on a hike without telling Mom and Dad?"

Sara lied, saying, "No, I wouldn't do that."

"You are more of an adventurer than that, I know you were thinking about it," replied Patrick.

"Okay... okay, so I was. But I was just going in to find more ingredients for us to use to make for breakfast since we used all of the ingredients yesterday morning. We used everything we harvest that day."

"Well, we better hurry before they wake up."

"Really?!" exclaimed Sara.

"Yes, let's just stay close and stay together."

"Yes, of course."

Sara and Patrick took off into the forest to gather more ingredients. They found more mushrooms, wild onions, and garlic to sauté and have with eggs and ham. Just as Sara and Patrick returned from the forest, they saw Mom and Dad setting up another fire to start cooking, with a look of agitation on their faces.

While back at camp, Mom and Dad woke up and discovered that Sara and Patrick were gone. It was unlike them to just take off without notifying anyone. Mom and Dad started searching for their children. After about ten minutes, Dad noticed their packs were still there, so he realized they couldn't be far, so he gathered firewood for the fire to make breakfast. Mom packed the gear for their day of fishing. Just as she finished, she sat by Dad and began to talk more about the road with the white house. "Do you think we can do some research on that house?" asked Mom.

Dad laughingly stated, "Of course, we can, research is what I do best. Besides, we need to get the tire fixed or get it replaced before we head out."

Right at that moment, Sara and Patrick emerged from the forest with the ingredients for breakfast. Mom and Dad turned their heads in unison with looks of frustration on their faces.

"Where have you two been?" Mom asked agitatedly.

Sara replied, "We are sorry, Mom, we went to get ingredients again for breakfast."

Patrick followed with, "We were hoping to be back before you woke up, it was going to be a surprise, we are sorry."

"Well, as long as you are safe. Just please let us know next time," replied Dad.

"Thank you for getting more ingredients, that is sweet of you," said Mom.

After breakfast, they finished packing their bags with fishing gear, lunch, and water and went on a hike to the creek to enjoy a day of fishing.

At the fishing spot they found, everyone unpacked the fishing gear and threw their lines in the water. As they sat there waiting for bites, Sara asked, "May we go to a library and research information on the house that we saw on the way here?"

"Your mom and I were just talking about that while you two were in the forest this morning," replied Dad.

"That is so cool, I would love to go visit a new library."

Dad said, "We will go to the library in the morning after we pack up and leave. There is one not too terribly far from here."

Sara thought how wonderful it will be to see a different library than the one in her hometown.

There was nothing wrong with the one at home. It would just be fun to see and explore something else new. For now, she was just going to concentrate on the task at hand, which was to enjoy the weather while fishing.

It was a beautiful day for fishing; there was a small cool breeze coming in from the north. The trees and flowers were in full bloom. The grass was a brilliant green, with wildflowers scattered within the grass. The birds were singing, and it sounded as if they were in harmony together, as if they were singing the same song. In the distance, squirrels running, chasing, and chattering at each other could be heard. Also in the distance, one could hear what might be deer rustling in the thicket. Overhead, a hawk and a bald eagle could be seen.

Patrick felt a tug at his line. "Ahhh!" yelled out Patrick, practically dropping the rod, from being startled.

He and Sara had never been fishing before. Dad coached him on how to reel it, "Pull back to set the hook, keep tension on the line and reel it in." Dad went on to say, "Congratulations, son! How does it feel to catch your first fish?"

Without realizing it, Patrick let out his little secret. "That was awesome. This adventure is kinda fun. Ohhh, I meant it was okay."

Patrick just landed his first fish. It was a decent-size perch. After a short while, Patrick leaned over to Sara and asked her if she wanted to explore more trails.

Sara was the first to speak up. "Hey, Mom, Dad, may Patrick and I go explore more trails? We won't go far, and we will be back shortly."

"I don't know," said Mom. "This forest is vast, but the trails are looped, so if you stay on the trail, then it will lead you back to where we are."

Patrick replied with, "We promise to stay together and not get lost. And we will pack out what we take in. We also have plenty of water."

"Well, I suppose you did make it back from your morning hike with more ingredients for breakfast..."

Sara and Patrick looked at their mom in anticipation for the answer they wanted to hear.

"Okay, just be safe," Mom replied.

"Thank you, Mom, we will," Patrick and Sara replied.

"Don't forget, we are going to the library in the morning to research the area and that old house," Dad added.

"We won't," said Sara. "Let's go, Patrick," Sara continued.

Sara and Patrick took off onto the trail.

CHAPTER 7

"Wow, it is so pretty here, I wish we could just stay," said Sara.

"That would be cool, there are other neat places as well. Some people will probably think where we live would be neat as well," replied Patrick.

While walking along the trail, a narrow path appeared off to the side. It was covered in grass with a shallow blanket of leaves and some debris from trees and brush.

"Let's explore this trail," said Sara.

Patrick replied, "That looks like an animal trail, cool, but that would be neat to see wild animals up there."

"I would love to see wild animals in the woods, in their natural habitat."

"This doesn't look like it's too safe, though, but if animals go in and out, it can't be all that dangerous."

"So are we going?"

"Yes, let's do it."

"Awesome!" exclaimed Sara.

Sara and Patrick headed for the game trail; the trail was a bit overgrown and a little difficult to maneuver into. The brush was dense with thick vines going up the trunks of huge walnut and oak trees. After about an hour or so of hiking on the game trail, the passage was too thick to continue any further.

Sara and Patrick tried to make their way out, they got turned around and headed into a denser part of the forest. While traversing the terrain and navigating around thick brush and trees, Sara and Patrick found themselves off the original game trail they had entered. Sara and Patrick saw a clearing up ahead. The clearing opened up into a beautiful wide meadow, with tall grasses and wildflowers.

"I know we didn't pass this on the way into the woods. Where are we?" asked Sara.

"I don't know," replied Patrick.

"Do you have a map?" asked Sara.

"No, I thought you might have one."

"OH NO! Mom has a map. We didn't get one."

"Well, I do have a phone."

"No signal, remember?"

"Well, maybe I can get something here, doesn't hurt to try," said Patrick.

Sara started to yell, "HELP!"

"We are out in the middle of nowhere, do you really think someone will hear?"

"It won't hurt, do you have any better ideas?"

"Yes, I once heard that moss grows on the north side of the tree."

"Oh, so do you know which direction the trail is from here?" asked Sara.

"The whole trail is a loop, so if we simply keep walking in the same direction, then we will eventually end back up on the trail."

"Okay, let's start walking, I guess." Sara cried out again, "HELP!"

"Shhh," Patrick said in a low whispering voice.

"What's—"

"Shhhh, hush," Patrick interrupted Sara abruptly. "I just saw movement, it went right behind that tree," Patrick continued in a whisper.

They slowly started to approach where Patrick saw movement.

Walking lightly and just a mere whisper, they arrived at the spot where Patrick saw movement.

"What are we looking for, Patrick?" Sara said in a low whispering voice.

"What was moving," replied Patrick.

"What do you think it was?"

"I don't know."

"Oh, could it—"

Sara froze midsentence. She saw the tall, thin man standing right in front of her. Patrick's back turned to them. A cold chill ran down her spine, the little hairs on the back of her neck stood straight up. She could not so much even let out a small silent whisper. So screaming was impossible. In her head, she let out the loudest scream she had ever yelled. But nothing was able to escape her vocal cords. She stood there motionless and in shock, looking at the man she had only seen hiding behind the signs. Finally, she had come face-to-face with the man who had scared her twice before. Now it was surreal, it was like a bad nightmare from which she could not wake from.

Patrick was overlooking the area at which he saw the movement. He couldn't see nor hear anything, including what Sara started to say. Patrick, while overlooking the area directly in front of him, saw more movement in the distance. He focused on one spot in the thicket; the animal emerged from behind the thick midlevel brush. It is a stout handsome twelve-point buck with antlers expanding the arm reach from fingertip to fingertip of a full-grown adult man.

"Sara, I think I see what was moving earlier. Look, he is so big and pretty... Sara? SARA!"

Patrick turned around to see that the tall, thin man was standing right in front of Sara. Patrick started to yell. The tall, thin man interrupted Patrick before he could make a sound.

In a gruff low voice, the man said, "Don't be scared, it looks like you two have made your way off the trail. I heard you yell for help. It seems like you two just might be lost. Let's get you back to your parents."

"Wait. What?" said Patrick.

"I thought you were going to hurt us," said Sara.

While laughing, the man replied, "Hurt you? What makes you think I would do that?"

"Who are you?" asked Patrick.

"Anymore, I am just an old man, scavenging, fishing, and hunting for food to make ends meet. I am a fur trader," stated the man.

"You were hiding behind the signs. I screamed when I saw you. I thought that was creepy," said Sara.

"I had just come out of the woods and saw your car. I waited for you to turn around and tried to flag you down and ask if you needed directions," explained the man.

"That does explain some things," Sara replied.

"Let's get you out of the woods and back on the trail to your parents," said the man.

"We were fishing in the creek, where it is closest to the trail," explained Patrick.

"I think I might know right where your parents are then. That is my favorite place to fish," said the man.

CHAPTER 8

The trio headed out of the woods on their way back to Sara and Patrick's mom and dad. Patrick nor Sara realized they were so deep in the woods, the trek seemed like it was taking hours. Sara, Patrick, and the man were getting hungry. As they stopped to take a snack break, the man started to talk about the area they were hiking through. The snack consisted of wild strawberries, wild blackberries, and persimmons harvested from the surrounding plants.

"This forest is massive, there are a lot of resources available to those who know what to look for and how to find them. There is a lot of wild edible vegetation, nuts and fruit. There is also a lot of game to hunt. By the way, how did you two manage to get so lost?" asked the man.

"We followed a narrow path that connected to the main trail, it wasn't too bad at first, but the further we kept walking, the harder it was to hike. It looked like an animal trial," replied Patrick.

"Oh, what you are referring to is called a game trail, you probably followed it back to the bedding area," replied the man.

"I did see a large deer behind some brush, his antlers were huge," said Patrick.

"His antlers are not even fully grown yet, they won't be 'til late summer. There are also other wild game here, like quail, grouse, and pheasant. Some other animals that might interest you are the rabbits, squirrels, and bobcat. There are a lot more than just those as well."

"There are a lot of plants and animals here to see and enjoy. This place is so beautiful. It is so amazing that anyone can come see all this beauty and enjoy all the recreational activities it has to offer," said Sara.

"Hey, we are heading north, I can tell because moss is growing on the side of the tree that we are traveling," said Patrick.

"Yes, we are heading north, but keep in mind that moss grows on the side of the tree that is the wettest and darkest side of the tree, which just so happens to be on the north side of the tree where we are. So you may see the majority of the moss growing on any part of the tree depending on the growth of the brush and canopy," replied the man.

"How do you know so much?" asked Sara.

"I have been living here for a very long time," replied the man.

The trio continued on the hike back to the fishing spot where Sara and Patrick's parents were waiting for them to return. Meanwhile, back at the fishing spot, Mom and Dad were talking about how long the children had been gone. They were trying not to worry. However, they had been gone for hours now.

"I wonder where the children are," said Mom.

"I am sure they are into mischief and having a blast," replied Dad.

"I didn't know Patrick knew so much about nature, he must have read about it in a book, or maybe he studied it in school. He is on his computer and phone a lot, maybe he watches online nature videos," said Mom.

Just at that moment, Patrick and Sara appeared out of the woods.

"There you two are! Where have you been? It is getting late," said Mom.

"We were exploring, we got turned around, we are fine. We had help getting back," said Sara.

"Who helped you?" asked Mom.

"The man right behind us," Sara replied.

"There is no one there," replied Dad.

Sara said, "What? He is standing right—" As she turned around, Sara noticed the man was not there. "What? Where did he go?" Sara continued to ask.

"We didn't see him," Mom said, confused.

"He is like a ghost, one second he is there, the next he is gone," Sara said.

"It was the same guy we saw standing behind the signs," replied Patrick.

"Wait! What? So you saw him too then?" asked Sara.

Sheepishly, Patrick responded with, "Y... e... s..."

"You made me think I was going crazy this whole time!" Sara yelled at Patrick.

"I am sorry, sis. I know it was wrong, I just feel like sometimes I am in your shadow, and I am not as successful as you. I am sorry," replied Patrick. Patrick continued with, "We did learn a lot more from the man, which I thought was cool."

"That was cool. But do you know what would be even more cool? When we go to the library and learn even more about the general area," Sara said in an antagonistic way.

"We will be going to the library in the morning after breakfast and we get packed up," Dad said abruptly, ending the argument.

"Let's pack up and head back to camp," Mom said. She continued with, "It sounds as if you two had a long day."

Everyone gathered up all the gear and headed back to camp. They found their way back to camp just as night fell, so Dad grilled some hot dogs, heated up baked beans, and with a small side salad, the dinner was satisfying. As everyone finished dinner, they were tired and getting ready to go to bed. A high-pitched scream in the distance was heard, startling everyone. They were not used to hearing such sounds in the wild. The family was concerned about someone being hurt. The scream sounded like a young girl but different.

"Should we all go check it out?" Mom asked.

At that moment, they heard the same sound but from a different direction. In the sky, under the moonlight, they saw a large bird flying overhead. It looked like it was carrying something.

"It looks like a large bird caught some prey," Patrick announced.

"Let's all get some sleep, we have a busy day tomorrow," said Dad.

"Okay, good night, everyone, I am excited about the library!" Sara exclaimed.

The night was peaceful and quite after the owls had hunted and caught their prey. There was the same sound of crickets, cicadas, frogs, and other nocturnal creatures. A slight breeze swept over the grass and other plants. The night air seemed a bit cooler and more moist than usual summer weather. Clouds were coming in, hiding the moon and cooling off the warm summer air. As the sun rose, the moisture from the cool night air condensed, and the dew collected on the blades of grass gave moisture to the plants and insects. Patrick and Sara had a good night's rest and were excited about visiting the library to find more information on the area. As vast as the area was, there was an inclusive history of itself, not just in parts.

Patrick was the first to wake and started packing up the camp and cleaning the campground. Sara, soon to rise after Patrick, followed behind him in packing and cleaning the campsite. Mom and Dad said, "We pack out what we bring in." They decided to take it one step further and cleaned up more than what they just packed in. By the time Mom and Dad woke up, the campsite and surrounding area had been cleaned up of all litter, and their tents and bags were packed and ready to load up in the SUV.

"Well, good morning, Sara, good morning, Patrick!" Mom said excitedly.

"Good morning, Mom, good morning, Dad," replied Sara.

"We can help pack up your tent and the rest of the bags and supplies," said Patrick.

"Great job on cleaning up the campsite, if everyone cleaned it as well as you two did, the park and all the natural environments would remain in pristine condition."

After everything had been gathered and collected, the gear and supplies were loaded into the SUV and they headed into town. The road which they traveled on to get to the campsite looked far different from when they first traveled on it so late in the evening. The gravel road looked far more inviting, less mysterious. The trees looked like they have restrained from trying to reach out and grab them and pull them into the forest. The shadows were not looming over them and dancing as if trying to hide what was in the wilderness to grab them and keep them lost. The forest was still just as dense as when they first arrived, but it was, by far, more appealing.

Chapter 9

As they arrived into town, they saw a small little diner that was serving breakfast. Dad pulled the SUV into a parking spot, everyone got out, and as they walked toward the entrance into the restaurant, the smell of bacon, eggs, and pancakes filled the air. The family entered the restaurant, got seated, and placed their order. The idea of a tall stack of pancakes appealed to Sara. While eggs and omelets were great, the sound of eggs were just not that appetizing. Sara preferred change as opposed to the same thing every time. She liked to think of that as the adventurer in her. Patrick, Mom, and Dad all placed the same order of eggs, bacon, wheat toast, and hash browns. Sara felt as if she had always been the oddball of the family. She related most with Mom. The conversation started with an agenda for the day: getting a new tire for the SUV.

"I am still concerned what happened on the way to the campground with the tire," said Sara.

"That part of the journey was startling. However, we overcame it, and we are getting the tire replaced today," replied Dad.

"While we are getting it replaced, I am concerned about the incident as well," stated Mom.

"That house was so creepy but also so cool. I wonder if it has ever been used for a haunted house," asked Patrick.

"I hope to find out more information on that house and the area around it as well," said Dad.

"I think we should start by asking someone at the circulation desk and looking at the periodicals, reviewing newspapers first," said Sara.

After breakfast, the family went to get a new tire for the SUV. The tire was punctured by a very sharp pointed object according to the mechanic. Sara and Patrick had startled looks on their faces as this information was revealed to everyone. Mom had already told Dad, but neither one had told Sara nor Patrick.

"What did you run over, a nail?" asked the mechanic.

"Is that what you saw in the rut in the road, Mom, a nail?" asked Sara.

"No, well, sorta, I might as well tell you. It was a broken piece of wood that was lying in the deepest part of the rut, making it impossible to see while driving. The broken piece of wood had nails all the way down it, making it impossible to avoid any nails."

"OHHH, WOW!" exclaimed Sara.

Patrick was thinking, *But we avoided it on the way out.* Also, he was thinking, *There has to be more to this story than we realize.*

The tired was replaced and put back into the SUV, and Dad drove off to the library.

At the library, sitting in one of the high-backed chair, "the man" was reading a book. The family walked into the library and headed straight to the circulation desk and asked for the periodicals. The periodicals were right next to where the man was sitting. Sara was the first to spot him.

"Hey, Patrick, look," whispered Sara.

Patrick whispered a reply, "Hey, it's the man, I wonder what he is doing here."

"I don't know, let's go find out."

"What about Mom and Dad?"

"We will introduce them to him later," replied Sara.

"Let's go say hi at least and thank him for guiding us back to Mom and Dad," said Patrick.

As Sara and Patrick approached the old man, the old man looked up and spotted the children with a perplexed look on his face. The old man started to get up but decided to slowly sit back down and wait for the children to come over to him. The old man was reading a book on history of the area, and next to him sat a table with a stack of nature books from different areas. It looked like the old man had been doing a lot of research.

"How are you?" asked Sara.

"Thank you," said Patrick.

"Just reading, you are welcome," said the old man.

"We came here to do some research as well," replied Sara.

"That house is so cool," Patrick added. "We want to learn more about the house," Patrick continued.

"What house?" asked the old man.

"The white house that we saw, where you were hiding behind the sign," replied Sara.

"Oh, my house, I was not trying to hide," the old man replied.

"UHHHH, your house?" asked Patrick in awe.

"Yes, my house. It has been in my family for generations, and it caught fire about ten years ago, and I have been working on refurbishing it for a long time. It still has some work that needs to be done on the inside. The patio and decks need a lot of work."

"So it is in construction right now. Oh, we are so sorry," said Sara.

"So that you are not trying to scare us," stated Patrick.

"Of course not. As I said before, I thought your family were lost, and I helped you to get back to your parents. So while I may seem like a scary old man, I am just a simple an old man trying to survive."

"We would like to introduce you to our mom and dad. Would that be okay?" asked Patrick.

"I guess," replied the old man.

Sara and Patrick ran off to go get their mom and dad.

"Hey, Mom, Dad, we would like to introduce you to someone we met!" Sara and Patrick exclaimed.

The family walked over to the area where the old man was sitting. As they rounded the corner, Sara and Patrick gasped. They did not see the old man.

"Where did he go now?" asked Sara.

"I don't know, he was just here," stated Patrick.

"He is good at this disappearing act."

"Was it the same old man we saw at the house?" asked Mom.

"Yes," replied Sara.

"Also the same man who helped us out of the forest," replied Patrick.

"Well, maybe he is just busy or just wants to be left alone," said Dad.

In place of the old man in the seat if the chair rested the very book he was reading. They approached the chair, and in the chair, the book was turned to the history of the very place where they had to turned around. Stuck in the pages was a newspaper clipping of the house. The headline read, "A FAMILY OF 4 PERISHES IN HOUSE FIRE." The article read there was a house fire in which a family of four was trapped in the house and had perished. In a separate article, it read that the community was giving effort to rebuild the house after generations of neglect.

"That house is old, I am glad to see they are repairing it. That is awesome that this area has such a rich and amazing history, along with the natural surrounding. We should come back here some time. Maybe the house will be completed," Dad said.

Everyone agreed.

"Where to next?" asked Sara.

"On our way to wherever we go, I will be playing my video game. I am so close to the next level, I can just picture it now," said Patrick.

"Oh, you and that stupid game. Haven't you learned anything yet?" Sara asked antagonistically.

And the next adventure awaits!

The 1.5 million-acre Mark Twain National Forest invites you to enjoy its many opportunities. Whether you are a sightseer, camper, hiker, backpacker, hunter, angler, picnicker, floater, bird watcher, horseback rider, biker, or all-terrain vehicle (ATV) user, the Forest has something special for you. Located in central and southern Missouri, the Mark Twain is traversed by rivers and streams, some fed by the largest springs in the country. The Forest extends from the St. Francois Mountains in southeast Missouri across the foothills and plateaus of the Ozarks to the glades and balds in the southwest.

Mark Twain, as all national forests, is managed for a variety of uses, including outdoor recreation, range, timber, wilderness, minerals, watershed and habitat for fish and wildlife. Managing for multiple-use distinguishes National Forests from National Parks. National Parks are managed with more emphasis on preservation of unique resources and on public uses compatible with that mission.

Mark Twain National Forest contains a wide variety of natural resources including woodlands of oak, hickory, pine and maple, oak savannas, rocky barren glades, and clear free flowing springs and streams. These resources provide a sustainable timber supply, minerals, recreation and a home to over 650 species of wildlife and fish.

Everyone is welcome, regardless of race, creed, color, sex, age or national origin. Write, call or stop by the Supervisor's Office or one of the field offices to discover what the Mark Twain National Forest has to offer. (See back cover for a list of offices).

Wilderness & Other Special Areas

The Mark Twain National Forest includes seven Congressionally-designated Wildernesses: Bell Mountain, Rock Pile Mountain, Irish, Paddy Creek, Hercules Glades, Devils

Backbone, and Piney Creek. Wilderness lands total more than 63,000 acres and are areas where the earth and its community of life are untrammeled by man, and may also contain ecological, geological, or other features of scientific, educational, scenic or historical value, with little evidence of humans. Hikers, backpackers, and horseback riders seek them out for peace and solitude. Hunting, fishing, and primitive camping are allowed, but wheeled vehicles and groups of more than 10 persons are not. Trailheads with limited parking spaces are located next to the Wildernesses.

The Mark Twain manages more than 73,600 acres as semi-primitive areas where the only access is by hiking, horseback or mountain bike, The Forest also manages about 258,600 acres for semi-primitive motorized recreation. These areas provide moderate to high opportunities for solitude. Hunting and fishing, with a valid state license, are permitted in these areas.

Semi-primitive areas differ from Congressionally-designated Wilderness in that resources, such as timber and wildlife, are deliberately managed.

Besides Wilderness and semi-primitive areas, the Mark Twain maintains about 30,600 acres as "special areas". These areas are managed for the protection of unusual environmental, recreational, cultural or historical resources, and for scientific or educational studies. Some special areas contain rare and endangered species of plants and animals.

Hunting, Fishing & Nature

The Mark Twain National Forest is popular with hunters, trappers, anglers and persons who enjoy observing, studying and photographing wildflowers and wildlife. The Forest has over 320 species of birds, 75 species of mammals and 125 species of amphibians and reptiles. Game species include whitetail deer, turkey, quail, woodcocks, doves, ducks, geese, rabbits, raccoons, squirrels, opossums, woodchucks, bobcats, and coyotes.

Except where posted otherwise, hunting and fishing with a valid Missouri license is permitted on National Forest lands.

Fishing is one of America's most popular pastimes. Mark Twain's streams and lakes contain over 200 species of fish, including bass, bluegill, sunfish, crappie, and catfish. Three of the Forest's spring-fed streams, Mill Creek, Spring Creek and Little Piney on the Houston-Rolla-Cedar Creek Ranger District, have wild rainbow trout populations. The Eleven Point National Scenic River on the Eleven Point Ranger District and the North Fork of the White River on the Ava-Cassville-Willow Springs Ranger District have sections stocked with Rainbow trout by the Missouri Department of Conservation. To possess trout, a Missouri trout stamp is required in addition to a Missouri fishing license. Some special regulations on size and limits apply. Lakes range in size from about 10 acres to the 440-acre Council Bluff Lake on the Potosi-Fredericktown Ranger District. Be sure to check bulletin boards for creel or length limits, and horsepower or other motor regulations. To preserve water quality, only electric motors are permitted on most of the lakes.

Camp and Picnic Areas

There are more than 40 campgrounds and picnic areas in Mark Twain. Campgrounds and picnic areas are usually located near a special attraction such as a spring. stream, lake, towering bluff or other scenic area. Float camps, only accessible by water, are available on the Eleven Point National Scenic River.

Campgrounds and picnic areas vary from a few table sites to developed campgrounds. Some have walks, trails, and restrooms that are handicapped-accessible. Camping fees vary, with special fees for group camping or use of pavilions. Many can be reserved by calling 1-877-444-6777 or at www.recreation.gov

Cool, Clear Streams

The Forest has more than 350 miles of perennial streams, most suitable for floating with canoes, kayaks, rafts, and inner tubes. Some, such as the St. Francis on the Potosi-Fredericktown Ranger District, have seasonal whitewater but may be too shallow for floating most of the year.

Floating offers close-up views of rocky bluffs, caves, springs, vegetation, birds, and other wildlife. Some favorite float streams are the Eleven Point National Scenic River, the Current, Big Piney, Gasconade, and North Fork Rivers.

The Forest Service and the Missouri Department of Conservation maintain river accesses on the most popular streams. Private outfitters are available in most of these areas. Where waterways pass through private lands, permission of the owners is required before using their lands for camping and picnicking.

Places to Hike & Ride

Mark Twain has hundreds of miles or trails, including over 250 completed miles of the 500-mile Ozark Trail. Starting near St. Louis, Missouri, the trail will wind over state, federal, and private lands extending to the Arkansas border. Plans are to connect the Missouri section with the 200-mile Ozark Highlands Trail in Arkansas. Go to www.ozarktrail.com for more info.

The Forest has three National Recreation Trails: Berryman Trail (part of the Ozark Trail) and Crane Lake Trail on the Potosi-Fredericktown Ranger District, and Ridge Runner Trail on the Ava-Cassville-Willow Springs Ranger District. All seven Congressionally-designated Wildernesses have hiking trails. Most recreation areas have hiking trails.

Bicycles and mountain bikes are generally permitted on trails but may be prohibited, such as in Wildernesses.

Motor vehicle users must comply with Missouri law. Motorized vehicles may be used only on open Forest roads or designated ATV trails. All other use of motor vehicles is prohibited. Trail bikers and ATV users ride the challenging trails at the Chadwick Motorcycle Use Area on the Ava-Cassville-Willow Springs Ranger District. The 80 miles of trails wind in and out of deep forested hollows and along ridge tops. Riders also ride the designated trails at Sutton Bluff Recreation Area on the Salem Ranger District. Permits are required to ride these areas. Overnight camping is available at nearby Forest recreation areas. Unlicensed ATVs and UTVs may only be ridden on roads if they have a current county permit valid in the county in which they are ridden.

Mark Twain National Forest has many trails and areas for horseback riding. Some of these are the Berryman on the Potosi-Fredericktown Ranger District, Cole Creek, Kaintuck, Cedar Creek, and Big Piney on the Houston-Rolla-Cedar Creek Ranger District, the Victory on the Poplar Bluff Ranger District, and the Blue Ridge on the Eleven Point Ranger District. Swan Creek area on the Ava-Cassville-Willow Springs Ranger District is a favorite riding area with an open field for grazing or overnight camping. Riders also can use several sections of the Ozark Trail and most forest roads.

Some Ideas for Scenic Drives

Although most roads through the Mark Twain National Forest are scenic, a few are outstanding. The scenery is especially attractive in mid-April to early May when redbud and dogwood bloom, and in mid-October to early November when leaves change color.

The Glade Top Trail (Forest Road 147) is a National Forest Scenic Byway. This 17 mile winding gravel road will take you through cedar dotted knobs on the Ava unit of the Ava-Cassville-Willow Springs Ranger District. Caney Picnic Area and other stops offer vistas of surrounding glades and northern Arkansas Mountains.

Blue Buck Knob National Forest Scenic Byway is 24 miles of paved highway on the Willow Springs Unit of the Ava-Cassville-Willow Springs Ranger District. The Byway starts south of Cabool on Hwy. 181, then east on Hwy. 76 to County AP south past Carman Springs Wildlife Refuge Management Area.

Sugar Camp Road National Forest Scenic Byway also offers ridge top views of Ozark scenery. Located on the Cassville Unit of the Ava-Cassville-Willow Springs Ranger District, the 28-mile forest drive runs along Highway 112 near Roaring River State Park, Forest Rd 197, and Highway 86 from Eagle Rock to Natural Bridge.

For more information...

Forest Supervisor
Mark Twain National Forest
401 Fairgrounds Rd
Rolla, MO 65401
Phone: (573) 364-4621
FAX: (573) 364-6844

**Ava-Cassville-Willow Springs
District Ranger**
P.O. Box 188
1103 S Jefferson
Ava, MO 65608
Phone: (417) 683-4428
FAX: (417) 683-5722

Eleven Point District Ranger
4 Confederate Ridge Road
Doniphan, MO 63935
Phone: (573) 996-2153
FAX: (573) 996-7745

**Houston-Rolla-Cedar Creek District
Ranger**
108 S Sam Houston Blvd
Houston, MO 65483
Phone: (417) 967-4194
FAX: (417) 967-2524

Poplar Bluff District Ranger
P.O. Box 988
1420 Maud St
Poplar Bluff, MO 63901
Phone: (573) 785-1475
FAX: (573) 785-0267

**Potosi-Fredericktown District
Ranger**
P.O. Box 188
Highway 8 West
Potosi, MO 63664
Phone: (573) 438-5427
FAX: (573) 438-2633

Salem District Ranger
P.O. Box 460
1301 South Main
Salem, MO 65560
Phone: (573) 729-6656
FAX: (573) 729-2867

References:

Mark Twain National Forest. United States Department of Agriculture Forest Service, www.fs.usda.gov. Accessed October 12, 2021.

Recreation.Gov. USA.gov, www.recreation.gov/camping/gateways/1086. Accessed October 12, 2021.

Brochures provided by: **Mark Twain National Forest Brochures**

Mark Twain National Forest - Maps & Publications (usda.gov)

Cedar Creek Trail (usda.gov)

About the Author

If I am not writing, I can be found exploring nature, fishing, hiking. I live real close to the lake of the Ozarks, surrounded by trees and a lake right across my house. I love spending time with my family. My fiancée is one of my best supporters. I thank her and my mom for all the support and encouragement. I also can be found in art galleries. I love to paint. I paint natural sceneries. I love to share ideas and support those who try. I have always said I will not tell a person they can't do something, I just ask that they have a backup plan. A person can do anything they put their mind and heart into.

About the Book

The first of a series about Sara and Patrick, along with their mom and dad visiting natural sites in the United States, the first stop being Mark Twain National Forest. Along the way, they find a mysterious old house and get lost in the deep forest. On the way, they learn how to help and work with each other and more so later. We will have to wait to see where the adventure goes next.

9 781962 497572